THIS WALKER BOOK BELONGS TO:

_____

_____

_____

_____

For David
with love
S.H.

First published 1990 by Walker Books Ltd
87 Vauxhall Walk, London SE11 5HJ

This edition published 2003

2 4 6 8 10 9 7 5 3

Text © 1990 Sarah Hayes
Illustrations © 1990 Barbara Firth

The right of Sarah Hayes and Barbara Firth to be identified as author and
illustrator respectively of this work has been asserted by them in accordance with
the Copyright, Designs and Patents Act 1988

This book has been typeset in Garamond Book

Printed in China

British Library Cataloguing in Publication Data:
a catalogue record for this book is available from the British Library

ISBN 0-7445-9456-1

The Grumpalump

Sarah Hayes illustrated by Barbara Firth

WALKER BOOKS
AND SUBSIDIARIES
LONDON • BOSTON • SYDNEY

The bear stared at the grumpalump.
The lump grumped.

The bear stared and
the cat sat on the grumpalump.
The lump grumped.

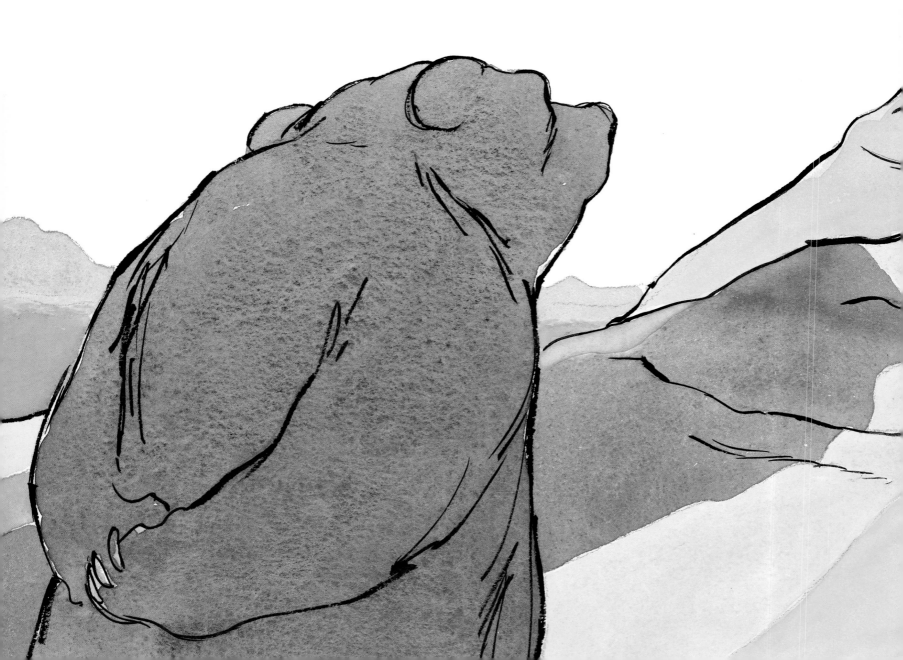

The bear stared, the cat sat and
the mole rolled on the grumpalump.
The lump grumped.

The bear stared, the cat sat, the mole rolled and the dove shoved the grumpalump. The lump still grumped.

The bear stared, the cat sat,
the mole rolled, the dove shoved and
the bull pulled the grumpalump.
The lump still grumped.

The bear stared, the cat sat, the mole rolled,
the dove shoved, the bull pulled and
the yak whacked the grumpalump.
The lump still grumped.

The bear stared, the cat sat, the mole rolled,
the dove shoved, the bull pulled,
the yak whacked and
the armadillo used it for a pillow.
But the lump still grumped.

Then
the
gnu
blew.

The lump grew plump, and got humps and
bumps, bits and bobs and
interesting knobs, and wings and
things attached with strings.
And still the gnu blew.

Then, to everyone's surprise,
the grumpalump began to rise.

The gnu drew breath
and clambered in.
The grumpalump began to grin.
"I'm off on a trip in my hot airship,"
said the gnu, and flew.
Absolutely true.

And how the bear stared.